This book belongs to

Jack and the Giant

A Story Full of Beans

Jim Harris

rising moon
Books for Young Readers from Northland Publishing

Thanks for the long-suffering help and advice of Stephanie and my wife, Marian.

Composed in the United States of America
Design and hand lettering by David Jenney
Edited by Stephanie Bucholz
Production supervised by Lisa Brownfield

Manufactured in Hong Kong by South Sea International Press Ltd.

FIRST IMPRESSION
ISBN 0-87358-680-8

Library of Congress Catalog Card Number pending

0632/30M/9-97

This book

is dedicated to David Jenney,

the Brooks Robinson

of art directors.

This is going to need a lot of ketchup.

ONCE THERE WAS A YOUNG COWPOKE NAMED JACK, who lived with his ma, Annie Okey-Dokey, on a dusty little desert ranch.

A no-good giant had stolen all the cattle off their ranch, the Bar None. All they had left was an old milk cow named Fred.

One night as they ate their supper, Annie said, "Jack, we're fresh out of food and money. You'll have to take Fred to town tomorrow and sell her."

The next morning, Jack and Fred hit the trail just as the sun cleared Bad Luck Butte. Along the way, Jack met a peddler with a creaky old wagon.

"Howdy, stranger," the peddler said. "That's some cow you've got there! Want to sell her?"

"Sure," Jack answered. "I'm on my way to the market right now."

"Why not sell her to me and save yourself a long trip into town?" the man asked. "I'll give you this bag of magic beans and this great-tastin' gum."

"Is there any flavor left in it?" asked Jack.

"You bet! I've only been chewin' on it for three weeks."

So the peddler headed off with Fred. Jack went home with the bag of beans, chewing his gum.

When Jack showed the beans to his ma, she was furious. "Oh, Jack!" she cried. "Your first cattle drive and you lose the whole herd!" And she chucked the beans out the window.

When Jack woke up the next morning, a leaf the size of a hay wagon was poking through his window. A huge beanstalk had grown up right beside the house.

Quick as a wink, Jack pulled on his boots and his Stetson hat and started climbing up the stalk. Jack climbed and climbed until he was eye-to-eye with elf owls and Harris hawks and even a desert thunderstorm. At last he poked his head through a cloud.

To his surprise, there in the clouds was a cow munching on grass. Off in the distance, Jack saw an adobe castle. By now, his stomach was growling like an old grizzly, so he headed straight for the castle, hoping for some real grub.

I hope they have giant mice. I'm starved!

He walked up to the castle and knocked on the door. A cook as big as a windmill answered. "You look like you might be hungry," he said, friendly as could be. "Come on in and I'll fix you some lunch."

"That would sure be nice, if you think nobody would mind," Jack answered.

"Oh, no," laughed the cook, "the giant just loves to have people for lunch."

Giant? Jack thought. But he was hungry enough to eat his boots, so he followed the cook inside.

Just as Jack was fixing to take his first bite, the giant stomped in through the front door.

Jack had seen the giant's face before—on a wanted poster! He was Wild Bill Hiccup, the famous cattle rustler, and he was ugly enough to peel the paint off a picket fence.

"If I can catch that yellow-bellied coyote," Jack thought, "I'll get a lollapaloozer of a reward!"

Suddenly Wild Bill pinched his nose and roared,

"Yippee yi yay,
Yippee yi yeeew
I smell the boots
of a buckaroo!"

MOM

But I've already had a bath this month.
GIANT DILLS
INGREDIENTS: CUCUMBERS, H2O, VINEGAR, SNAILS TOES, BIRD TEETH FER A PRESERVATIVE.

"Quick!" whispered the cook to Jack. "Hide, or he'll make a sandwich out of you." And he dropped Jack into a jar of pickles.

The giant looked everywhere for Jack. Finally, he gave up, sat down at the table, and started wolfing down his supper.

While the giant was eating, the cook brought in an old raggedy trunk and set it on the table. The giant pulled out a lasso, a banjo, and a furry buffalo.

Golden fries! Great idea!

He took the lasso and looped it over some french fries.

POP! FIZZLE! BANG!

"I'll be hornswiggled!" Jack gasped. The lasso had turned the fries to gold!

The giant bellowed, "Buffalo, buffalo, lay some gold, great big chunks that I can hold!" Soon, mounds of solid gold buffalo chips piled up on the table.

Wild Bill rubbed his eyes. "Banjo," he yawned, "all this money makes me tired. Sing me to sleep or else you're fired." Before long, the giant was snoring loud enough to give a rock a headache.

Jack plucked up his courage and stepped out from behind a chocolate shake. "Reach for the sky, Hiccup!" he shouted. "I've got you surrounded!"

The giant's eyes popped open and he jerked his hands high in the air. But then he spied Jack and grinned—a greasy, growly grin that slithered into a sneer.

Jack laughed nervously. "Well, uh, good joke, huh, Mr. Hiccup? But I think I hear my ma calling . . . yeah . . . so I'd better hit the trail."

Then, quicker than a snake can spit, Jack scooped up the banjo and the lasso, leaped onto the buffalo, and galloped out the front door like his life depended on it (which it did).

Now I know what fast food feels like.

The giant let out a roar that shook the castle and shattered glass. "Thief, thief!" he cried.

Jack felt the cloud shake and quake as the giant pounded closer and closer. By the time he reached the beanstalk, Jack could smell Wild Bill's breath behind him. **P.U.!!!**

Jack wrapped his legs around the buffalo and tightened his grip on his hat, and they jumped right off the cloud. Jack's Stetson billowed out like a parachute. They floated to the desert floor, landing with a gentle THUMP.

Wild Bill was climbing down the beanstalk when Jack grabbed a rope and lassoed a stout leaf. He tied the other end of the rope to the buffalo and gave him a gentle slap on the rump, yelling,

"GIDDY UP!"

The buffalo pulled the beanstalk until it was bent like a huge upside-down "U." Then Jack tipped his hat to the giant and cut the rope.

Have a nice trip. See you next fall.

WANG!

Shoooosh!

"Yeaaaiiiiiiooooooo!" cried the giant. He flew through the air and skidded across the desert, leaving a trail of chaps, jeans, boots—and the granddaddy of all canyons.

Jack showed his ma the wonderful treasures. She was so happy she cried.

Pretty soon the Bar None was the biggest, fanciest spread west of the Mississippi. Jack bought back Fred. And they all lived as happily as a herd of javelinas in a patch of prickly pear. (Though sometimes Jack got a little carried away with the golden lasso.)

JIM HARRIS began his career in North Carolina at the age of ten months with primitive but promising abstracts, using baby food as paint and his high chair tray as a canvas.

His work has appeared in numerous national magazines, at least as many as his parents left lying around open. Some magazines, such as *Ranger Rick* and *Sesame Street,* have actually printed his illustrations on purpose.

Among Jim's honors and awards are a silver medal from the New York Society of Illustrators and an Award for Excellence from the prestigious *Communication Arts* magazine competition. He is also a finalist in the Publishers Clearing House Sweepstakes.

Jim has illustrated over a dozen children's books and has a few more to finish before he can go out and play.